For Karen and Ems, with love – M.S.
For Dexter, with all my love – H.G.

Kelpies is an imprint of Floris Books
First published in 2019 by Floris Books
Series concept and illustrations © Floris Books 2019
Text © 2019 Michelle Sloan
Michelle Sloan and Hannah George have asserted their rights
under the Copyright, Designs and Patent Act 1988
to be identified as the Author and Illustrator of this Work

The publisher acknowledges subsidy from
Creative Scotland towards the publication
of this volume

 Also available as an eBook

British Library CIP data available
ISBN 978-178250-592-1
Printed & bound by MBM Print SCS Ltd, Glasgow

 Floris Books supports sustainable forest management
by printing this book on materials made from wood that
comes from responsible sources and reclaimed material

MIX
Paper from
responsible sources
FSC® C117931

The Baby Otter Rescue

Written by
Michelle Sloan

Illustrated by
Hannah George

Young
Kelpies

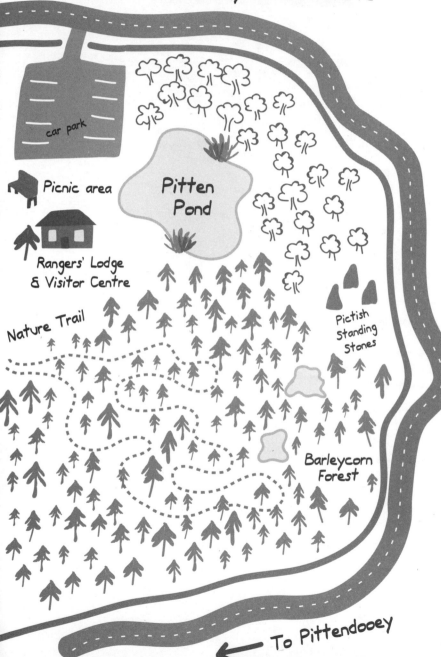

Entrance to Pittendooey Nature Reserve

car park

Picnic area

Rangers' Lodge & Visitor Centre

Pitten Pond

Nature Trail

Pictish Standing Stones

Barleycorn Forest

To Pittendooey

1

Isla MacLeod was looking at Pittendooey Nature Reserve rangers' lodge in a whole new way: upside down! *This is giving me a bat's-eye view*, Isla thought. *I can't wait for Buzz, Gracie and Lexi to have a go.* Isla and her friends were the Animal Adventure Club and they came to Pittendooey Nature Reserve three afternoons a week to help the head ranger, Lisa. They all loved nature, and looking after animals who needed help.

The door opened and in dashed a very wet Gracie. She stopped and stared at Isla, who was sitting backwards on the armchair with her legs held up high and her head hanging down. "Isla, what are you doing?" she asked.

"I'm pretending to be a bat," said Isla, "so I can learn more about them for our Bat Chat. It's on our To Do list." Isla swung herself upright again and, when the room had stopped spinning, pointed at the notepad lying open in front of her on the floor.

1. Research bats for the Bat Chat.
2. Practice bat origami activity.
3. Help Lisa tidy up the storage shed.

"Oh yeah, the Bat Chat!" cried Gracie as she hung up her dripping coat. "What have you learned so far?"

"That it's really hard to stay upside down! Did you know that bats' claws grip even when they're sleeping?"

"Otherwise they'd fall on their heads," said Gracie, and then she grinned. "Are you planning on making our Bat Chat visitors stand on their heads too?"

"Only if they want to," Isla giggled.

"But let's start by telling them about where bats live and what they eat."

"I can't wait for the Bat Walk into Craggy Woods at dusk," said Gracie. "Lisa's coming to supervise, but she said we could lead it."

"Your hair's drenched, Gracie. Is it *still* raining?"

"Yup," said Gracie. "When will it end? It's been pouring non-stop for days." She walked over to the kitchen area and grabbed a towel to squeeze water out of her hair. "I hope it stops before the Bat Chat. Do bats even come out when it's raining?"

"I don't know," said Isla. "We can look it up. Come on, let's find out more bat-tastic facts on the computer."

Isla and Gracie were looking at different types of bats when Lisa arrived. She closed the door and shivered. "Hi,

Animal Adventure Club," she said. "How's the Bat Chat preparation coming along?" She was just hanging up her wet things when the door flew open again.

"We are SOAKED!" boomed a loud voice.

"Could that be Lexi, my shy and quiet niece?" joked Lisa.

Lexi grinned. "That's me! And that's one very wet Pittendooey Nature Reserve patrol finished," she added.

"You're starting to steam!" said Isla, coming over to help Lexi take off her wet jacket.

"Ew, even my socks are soaking," complained Lexi. "Stick the kettle on, Buzz, I need a hot chocolate!" She frowned and looked around. "Where's Buzz gone? He was right behind me a second ago."

"That's funny," said Gracie. "I didn't see him. Oh well, I'll make the hot chocolates." She put the kettle on. "I was sure we had a new packet of biscuits in here," she said, rummaging around in the cupboards, "but there are just some crumbs and an empty wrapper."

Just then, Buzz arrived.

"There you are!" said Lexi. "I thought you'd vanished!"

Buzz laughed nervously. "Sorry, um... I just got held up for a minute."

"Anything interesting to report from your patrol?" asked Lisa.

"Yes," said Buzz, heaving at his welly boots. "The burn in Drookit Dell has burst its banks, so the Boggy Burn is now officially the Boggy Pond."

"I wonder how all the animals on the

reserve are coping with this rain?" asked Isla, helping Gracie to carry over the mugs of hot chocolate.

"Well," said Lisa, "some animals might struggle to find food. And some might even lose their homes if there are floods. We'll need to look out for any creatures that need our help. But the good news is that the boggy ground around the burn will be acting like a big sponge, soaking up lots of floodwater and stopping it streaming down the hill towards Pittendooey."

"Wow!" said Buzz. "I hadn't thought of that."

Suddenly Isla's phone began to ring. She pulled it out of her pocket and stepped away from the group to answer it.

"Perhaps we should add a flood action plan to our To Do list," suggested Lexi.

"Nice idea!" said Lisa.

"That was my mum," said Isla, coming back over to join the others. "The River Dooey has burst its banks, so the main road from Strathdooey to Pittendooey is completely flooded. She says there's no way through."

"Oh no!" said Gracie. "How is your mum going to get home from work at the health centre?"

"Well," said Isla with a smile, "she's called your mum and arranged for me to stay at your house for the night!"

"Ooh, a sleepover!" said Gracie.

Suddenly something small and furry darted across the floor, right past Lisa's outstretched foot. She shrieked and spilled her hot chocolate all over the To Do list.

"Did you see that?" asked Lexi. "A mouse!"

"It's disappeared through a wee hole under the sink," said Isla, fetching a cloth to mop up the spill.

"At least we know who ate all the biscuits," said Gracie.

"Urgh, mice!" Lisa shuddered and covered her face with her hands.

Buzz looked puzzled. "I thought you loved animals, Lisa. What's wrong with mice?"

"Buzz, I'll let you in on a little secret," said Lisa. "I love spiders, snakes and every type of beastie, creature and creepy-crawly you can imagine... But I'm absolutely terrified of *mice!*" She let out another scream, a pretend one this time. Isla, Lexi and Gracie laughed, but Buzz frowned.

"Well, I like them," he muttered.

"Let's start a new To Do list, Isla," said Lisa. "Number one: catch that mouse and find it a new home!"

2

"It's *still* raining," groaned Isla, looking out of Gracie's kitchen window that evening.

"And the water from the river is creeping closer," said Gracie.

Gracie's cottage was in the countryside just outside Pittendooey, near the nature reserve and very close to the river. Even in the fading daylight, Isla and Gracie could see the water flowing at an alarming speed. Large pools had formed in the fields nearby and the trees seemed to grow out of the water.

"If it carries on raining tomorrow, we'll need to put sandbags round the house to stop the water getting in," said Gracie's dad, opening the fridge for some milk. Just at that moment, Isla heard a series of shrill squeaks.

Gracie rolled her eyes. "Whenever we open the fridge, Haggis thinks it's feeding time."

"He's one greedy guinea piggy," said Gracie's mum, coming into the kitchen.

Gracie went over to the fridge too and rummaged inside. She found some cucumber and spinach leaves and popped them in a bowl. Then she flipped open Haggis's crate and carefully lifted him out onto the kitchen table. They all sat and watched him nibble his dinner.

"He's lucky to be snug and warm in here," said Isla. "But what about those poor animals out there in the rain?" She wandered back over to the window and pressed her nose against the cold surface. Her breath steamed up the glass and she rubbed it away with her finger. "I wonder where I'd go to keep safe?"

"Up a tree," suggested Gracie. "That would be easy if you were a bird or a squirrel."

"But not so easy for a badger or a rabbit," Isla pointed out. "Their homes will be flooded. And what about baby animals?"

"Poor wee things," said Gracie. "Thank goodness our home isn't flooded."

"Well, you never know," said Isla. "Maybe we'll have to climb a tree too!"

"I could build us a brilliant treehouse!" said Gracie, who was an expert den-builder. "Mind you, if it gets really stormy tonight, there might not be many trees left standing."

"Oh, don't say that!" said Isla.

"Don't worry, Isla," said Gracie's mum. "Gracie's just being dramatic. I looked at the weather forecast and the rain's due to stop tomorrow afternoon. Soon everything will be back to normal, your mum will be back home, and all the animals will be fine." She kissed the top of Gracie's head and ruffled Isla's hair. "Come on, you girls need to get to bed. It's getting late."

"Here," said Gracie's dad, handing them a mug each. "Take your warm milk up with you."

"Thanks, Dr Munroe," said Isla wrapping her fingers around the mug. "Goodnight, other Dr Munroe," said Isla to Gracie's mum. Gracie's mum was Pittendooey's local GP, and her dad was a GP too at Strathdooey Health Centre, where Isla's mum worked as a nurse. Luckily, today was his day off, so he wasn't stranded too.

Gracie's mum had made up a camp bed for Isla in Gracie's cosy bedroom. Isla loved Gracie's room. Her curtains had animal prints all over them. Isla could spot a squirrel, a badger and a hedgehog. There were posters of animals all over the walls too. Gracie had a large noticeboard and pinned on it were photos she'd taken of animal tracks and outdoor dens. There were survival tips and ideas for nature crafts and activities that she'd torn out of magazines too.

Sitting up under their duvets, the girls listened to the rain pounding on the window while they drank their warm milk.

"That is one sound I absolutely love," said Gracie, setting down her mug. "It's even nicer when you're in a tent all tucked up."

"Yes," said Isla quietly.

"Sleep well," yawned Gracie.

"You too," murmured Isla. She didn't

want to admit it to her friend, but all this rain was making her anxious. Her mum couldn't get home, Gracie's cottage might flood, and there were animals out there unable to find food or shelter. She closed her eyes tight and pulled the covers over her head to drown out the noise, wondering if sleep would ever come.

Isla wasn't sure how long she'd been asleep when she heard a sound. She opened her eyes and pulled the covers back. Gracie was snuggled up, and the rain was still pattering on the glass and the wind was howling, but then... there! Was that a soft little cry? She wasn't sure. *Perhaps it's the wind,* she thought. But then she heard the sound again.

It was more of a whine this time. *What if it's an animal in distress?*

"Gracie," Isla whispered. "Gracie, wake up!"

"What is it?" grumbled Gracie.

"I can hear something!"

"It's just the rain, go back to sleep," Gracie groaned.

Isla heard her turn over, and then she started snoring.

It was beginning to get light outside. Isla sat up, reached over to grab Gracie's dressing gown and slippers, and pulled back the curtain to peer into the early morning gloom.

She heard the whining sound again: it was definitely coming from outside, and now it was very close. Isla opened the window and thrust her head into the cool morning air. She looked over the soaking-wet fields and trees, but couldn't see anything. Then she heard it clearly: a loud mewing. Isla looked down, expecting to see a cat at the back door. She gasped. It wasn't a cat... It was a baby otter!

3

The otter cub's tufty dark-brown fur was wet and its tiny webbed toes poked out from under its tummy. Its long tail snaked along the soaking-wet ground. When it looked up and saw Isla, it let out another cry. It was very upset and frightened.

"Oh, you poor thing," whispered Isla. "You're just a tiny wee cub. Far too young to be without your mum."

Isla backed away from the window very slowly, over to Gracie's bed.

"Gracie, this time you have to wake up!" she said urgently.

Gracie stirred. "Too sleepy," she mumbled.

"I need your help! There's a baby otter at your back door."

Gracie shot up. "What?" she said. "An otter?" She scrambled out of bed and the two girls headed downstairs. They could hear the crying from the kitchen. Even Haggis the guinea pig looked alarmed, peering out of his crate anxiously.

As Gracie unlocked and opened the back door very carefully and slowly, the whining got a little louder. When the door was fully open, they saw the mewling cub looking up at them. "We need to keep very still and calm," whispered Isla. "So that the little cub knows it can trust us." The girls kept their breathing steady and soon the cub stopped squeaking. Then it flopped down on the step, keeping its eyes on them. The girls knelt down to observe the otter from a safe distance. It had a black button nose and whiskers that curved around its mouth.

"Oh my goodness," whispered Gracie. "I've never seen anything so cute. Lexi would love this!"

"It's adorable," Isla agreed, "and even cuter close up! But remember it's a wild animal. It's got very sharp little teeth and claws."

"True," said Gracie. "But where's its mum? I don't know much about otters, but this one doesn't look old enough to be out on its own."

The otter cub cocked its head to one side, as if it were listening intently to what they were saying. Then it let out another long, mournful wail.

"I wonder why it's come to your door?" asked Isla. "Maybe it's hungry and it smelled the fish fingers we had for tea last night!"

"Maybe," chuckled Gracie. "But I don't think we can give it fish fingers! What on earth should we feed you, wee chum?"

"You're right, I think it might be too young for fish. It's probably still having its mother's milk," said Isla.

"Its mum might be around somewhere," said Gracie, looking across her back garden. "Perhaps we should wait for the mum to come back for her baby."

"But if we leave it too long, the cub might get really, *really* hungry," said Isla.

"Or maybe it's not hungry after all. Maybe it's crying because it's injured," added Gracie. "Let's ask my mum and dad, they'll know what to do."

"Ask Mum and Dad what?" said Gracie's mum, coming into the kitchen looking very sleepy. "Why are you two up so early?" The baby otter mewled again and Gracie's mum clamped her hand to her mouth. "Oh my goodness, an otter! It's so cute!" she squealed.

"Yes, it's cute, but it's still a wild animal, Mum," said Gracie.

Isla chuckled. "Come on, Gracie, you were squealing about how cute it was yourself a minute ago!"

Gracie folded her arms. "Yes, but now we have to think sensibly and look after the otter. Think about our Animal Adventure Club code: 'Our mission is to take care of all living creatures.'"

The otter cub let out several squeaky whistles.

"Hmm," said Gracie's mum in her usual, sensible voice again. "I'm not sure what to do! Even though it's really early, I think you should call Lisa for help. This is an emergency, so she won't mind. Here, use my tablet to video call her," she said, picking it up from the kitchen table. "Then you can actually show her the otter."

Gracie touched the screen and waited for Lisa to answer.

"Gracie?" said a sleepy voice. Lisa's face appeared on the screen. She was bleary-eyed and her hair was very bushy. "This is an early call!"

"I know, I know," said Gracie. "Sorry, Lisa, but you'll understand when I show you why." Gracie flipped the camera to show Lisa the little otter.

"Ooh," cooed Lisa. "That is most definitely worth an early wake-up call!"

"What do you think?" said Isla. "What do we do? It just appeared at Gracie's back door."

"Well, by the looks of it, the cub is too small to be left alone," said Lisa. "And

Strathdooey Wildlife Hospital won't be able to get through because of the flood. It's up to us to look after this little otter cub. I'll head over with a cat box to put it in."

"What? Do you want me to keep it here?" asked Gracie's mum.

"No, don't worry," said Lisa with a chuckle. "We'll take it up to the nature reserve. There's a big crate and supplies for animals in the lodge."

"Were you worried you'd have an otter swimming around in the bath, Mum?" asked Gracie.

Gracie's mum giggled and raised her eyebrows. "To be honest, nothing would surprise me with the Animal Adventure Club, Gracie!"

4

Gracie messaged Buzz and Lexi to tell them about the otter, and they rushed round as soon as they could. By the time they arrived, the cub had been at Gracie's back door mewing for at least an hour. Everyone was creeping around the kitchen trying not to make too much noise, including Gracie's dad, who was making breakfast. The otter let out little wails from time to time. Haggis the guinea pig put his paws up to the bars of his cage and tried to squeak back.

"Aw! Haggis is trying to talk to him!" squealed Lexi. "And that cub is just SO

CUTE! I don't know if I can stop myself giving it a big squeeze. Buzz, hold me back!"

"I feel a bit guilty eating my breakfast while the little guy is so hungry," said Gracie's mum. "Poor baby."

"Me too," added Buzz, through a mouthful of fried-egg butty. "Great breakfast, Dr M."

"I wonder what Lisa will feed it?" mused Gracie's mum.

"It'll need special milk," said Buzz, who wanted to be a vet and knew lots about all sorts of animals. "I can go to the vet and see if they have any formula and a bottle."

"What's formula?" asked Lexi.

"Special powdered milk," said Buzz. "I think they feed baby otters the same milk they use for puppies."

"We'll have to look after this little otter all day! It's going to be a lot of work," said Gracie.

"YAY!" shouted Lexi. The otter squealed and backed away. Lexi bit her lip. "Oops, sorry little guy. I mean yay," she whispered.

Isla stared out at the countryside beyond the little otter. She couldn't help wondering how the cub had got there. She turned to the rest of the Animal Adventure Club. "While we're waiting for Lisa, why don't we look for the cub's mum? She might be nearby, but injured."

"Good idea," said Gracie. "Mum, Dad, can you keep an eye on our wee pal for a bit? We'll sneak out the front door and go round to the back garden that way, so we don't disturb it."

Isla, Lexi, Gracie and Buzz headed towards the swollen river at the very bottom of Gracie's garden. It was still raining, but the wind had died down. The clouds seemed to hang heavy in the sky, draped low over the trees and hills in the distance. Rooks cawed from their perches high above.

"Look, otter tracks," said Gracie, pointing to a cluster of paw prints in the soft mud near the river's edge.

"How do you know they're not fox or dog prints?" said Buzz. "They look dog-like to me."

"Because," said Gracie, pointing to the tiny prints with a long stick, "otter tracks have five toes and a large pad. Foxes and dogs only have four toes."

The gang peered closely and counted.

dog/fox prints

otter prints

Sure enough, there were five toeprints above the main pad. Buzz looked impressed at Gracie's tracking skills.

"But wait, there are lots of prints here. Did these all come from our baby otter?" asked Isla.

"Maybe its mum is here too!" cried Lexi.

"I don't think so," said Gracie. "Look at the prints again. What size are they?"

"They're all small," Lexi replied.

"Exactly," said Gracie. "There aren't any big paw prints, so that means the baby otter's mum isn't around. There's no spraint either."

"What's spraint?" asked Lexi.

"It's the poo of an adult otter," Gracie continued. "What a pity there isn't any here. I've always wanted to smell otter spraint."

Everyone looked at Gracie.

"Ew!" said Lexi, pinching her nose in disgust. "Why?"

"It's supposed to smell nice. Like jasmine tea actually," said Gracie with a grin.

"Let's look for other signs. Maybe the otters' holt is near here," suggested Isla.

"Their what?" asked Lexi.

"A holt is an otter's home," explained Isla. "It's usually in a burrow on the riverbank or in a hole in a tree trunk. And otters rest on a grassy 'couch' by the riverbed too. How cool is that?"

"Guys, look how high the water is," said Buzz. "The baby was probably flushed out of its holt and lost its mum."

Gracie pointed towards the track road that led to her house. "Look, that's Lisa's car," she said. "We'd better head back."

The Animal Adventure Club set off, but Isla held back for a moment, staring at the soaking-wet countryside around her. As she squinted into the distance, she thought she heard a tiny cry.

The baby otter! she thought. *But it can't be the cub: it's safe back at Gracie's house.*

The sound was probably just the wind, or the rush of the river. Yet Isla couldn't help feeling that the Animal Adventure Club had missed something important.

5

Lisa carried the otter cub in a cat box into the rangers' lodge at Pittendooey Nature Reserve. It was still mewing and whining. "Right, we need a hot-water bottle and towels and blankets for this wee thing," she told the Animal Adventure Club. "And we need to weigh him before we give him any milk, so we can work out how much he needs. Pop the kettle on please, Gracie."

"Is it a *he* then?" said Lexi.

"Yes," confirmed Lisa. "I checked and our cub is definitely a *he*."

"We'll need to think up a name for the wee toot," added Lexi.

Wearing thick gloves, Lisa carefully placed the cub in a basin and weighed him on the scales. "My friend who's a vet at Strathdooey Wildlife Hospital has been texting me with lots of advice," she said. "Judging by the cub's weight, we should give him milk every few hours, and maybe some mashed-up fish too. Now, we need to make up a bottle of formula. Buzz, can you help?"

Buzz and Lisa carefully added the right amount of powdered milk they'd got from the vet to the freshly boiled water. While it cooled, they moved the otter cub into the big crate in the lodge.

Isla gazed at the little furry creature. He sniffed around the crate, which was lined with blankets and towels, and then stopped and stared back at Isla.

He let out a long, contented sigh.

"He seems to like it in there," said Isla.

Buzz tested the temperature of the cooled formula by squeezing a few drops onto the back of his hand. "Perfect," he said. "Not too hot and not too cold."

Everyone crowded round to watch as Lisa opened the lid of the crate. The cub quickly worked out that there was tasty milk in the bottle and stood up on his two back legs, sucking and squeaking with delight. He stretched his tiny webbed paws around the sides of the bottle.

"You can each take a turn to feed him," said Lisa. "But we shouldn't let him have too much contact with humans. As cute as he is, he's still a wild animal."

The otter's fur was dry now and had fluffed up all over his little body.

"He really is the cutest fuzzball ever," said Isla.

"It's looks like he's trying to hold the bottle himself!" said Lexi, taking her turn to feed him.

"Keep the bottle tipped up so that the milk fills the teat," said Buzz to Lexi. "That way the cub won't gulp in air and get a sore tummy. I learned that from helping out with some puppies last year at the vet. And with my baby sister too!"

Lexi carefully lifted the bottle a little.

"When he's finished we should rub his back to burp him," said Buzz.

"Just like a baby," giggled Lexi.

"How long will we keep him here?" asked Isla.

"I can take him through to the wildlife hospital as soon as the road is clear," said Lisa. "I'm sure it won't be long."

"Maybe we should find a big tub for him to paddle in," suggested Lexi.

"When they're born, baby otters don't know how to swim. Their mothers have to teach them," said Isla, "so this wee guy probably can't swim very well yet."

"Maybe we can teach him," said Gracie.

"I've got some old armbands he could borrow!"

"Right now, this little one isn't ready for a swim; he's ready for a nap!" said Lisa.

After rubbing the cub's back until he burped, causing much laughter, Lisa closed the lid of the crate. Soon he began to look drowsy, and he curled into a ball in the blankets. Everyone stared at him as he slept. His little eyes were closed and he let out tiny snores.

"Adorable," sighed Lexi. "I'm going to sketch him while he's asleep." She went off to find her sketch pad.

Isla looked at the sleeping otter closely. "I think he looks a bit lonely," she said sadly.

Gracie frowned. "Do you think his mum is out there somewhere, trying to find him?"

"Maybe," said Isla thoughtfully. She couldn't shake off the feeling that she really *had* heard another animal down by the river. "Why don't we go out on patrol and have a look?"

"OK," said Gracie. "If we're careful and head round the lochside, we could do some mummy-otter tracking."

"Good idea," said Isla. "I'm going to grab my binoculars. Are you coming with us, Buzz?"

"Em, no, I think I'll stay behind." He took off his glasses and began rubbing his eyes. "I need to do some arts and crafts for the Bat Chat."

"I'll stay here and keep you company," said Lexi, who was walking back over with her sketch pad.

"Er, thanks..." Buzz mumbled, not looking

her in the eye. "And I really need to finish tidying the shed."

"But you've been doing that for the last two weeks!" said Gracie, zipping up her coat. "You must be nearly finished by now."

Buzz's face turned a little pink. "Oh, I know, it's taking ages," he said awkwardly. "I'll get there in the end."

Lexi peered curiously at him.

Something's up with Buzz, thought Isla, *and Lexi knows it too.*

"Well, Isla and Gracie, it's just the two of you. Be very careful out there," said Lisa. "Don't go too close to the water."

"Don't worry," said Gracie, "we'll be super-sensible." She slipped her foot into her boot and then let out a shriek.

"Not you again!" she said, tipping the

boot upside down. A mouse dropped to the floor. It gave Gracie an angry look and then bolted through a hole in the wall.

"I've never seen a mouse look so furious," said Isla with a chuckle.

"Not as furious as I'll look if that mouse doesn't go home soon!" squealed Lisa.

6

Isla and Gracie stepped outside. "Let's head towards Drookit Dell and the Boggy Burn," said Isla. "I want to see if the flooding is as bad as Buzz and Lexi said."

They trudged together along the path by Loch Dooey. Drizzle fell as a fine mist, glittering every leaf, blade of grass and eyelash.

"I'm soaked already!" laughed Gracie from under her hood.

Isla didn't answer. She was lost in thought.

"What's up, Isla?" Gracie asked. "You're

being very quiet. Are you worried about the baby otter?"

"Well, the thing is, I'm sure I heard another cry this morning, like the one our otter cub made, but further away," said Isla.

"Really?" said Gracie. "Why didn't you say?"

"I just put it to the back of my mind because we were so busy looking after the wee cub. But now I can't stop thinking about it. Maybe it *was* the mother otter."

"Or, it could've been another animal," suggested Gracie. "A fox or something."

As they walked along the lochside, the nature reserve seemed eerily quiet. Apart from the squelching of their feet on the sodden ground, there was no other sound.

When they arrived at the far side of the

reserve, the Boggy Burn looked just as Buzz and Lexi said: it was more like the Boggy Pond. The water level was so high that it was gushing and slopping over the slats of the little wooden bridge that led over the burn, making it too dangerous to cross. It wasn't the usual clear water they were used to seeing either. This flood water was brown and murky.

"I've never seen a flood like this before," said Gracie. "Let's walk a bit further and see if there's a safer place to cross."

They squelched down into the Drookit Dell.

"I don't think there's any way over to the other side," said Isla. "It's just a massive swamp!"

"Hang on," said Gracie. "Look, one of the trees has been blown down."

Sure enough, at the bottom of the dell a large Scots pine tree had crashed to the ground, creating a perfect bridge over the Boggy Burn. Gracie climbed up first and teetered across with her arms outstretched.

Loch Dooey

Picnic area

Rangers' Lodge & Visitor Centre

Pitten Pond

Nature Trail

boat sheds

Drookit Dell

Boggy Burn

"Take it steady," said Gracie to Isla, now following behind. "At least if you fall off here, you'll only land in mud."

By the time Isla made it across, Gracie was staring intently at the ground.

"What have you found?" Isla asked.

"Otter tracks again," Gracie said, turning to look at Isla with a beaming smile. "You were right, Isla! There *is* another otter. And it's been *here*."

They both knelt down to look at the paw prints in the squidgy mud. Isla knew what to look for now, so she peered closely and counted the toeprints.

Sure enough, each footprint was made up of five small ovals and the main pad.

But hang on a minute... she thought.

"Gracie, these are small: they're the same size as the tracks up by your house."

Gracie looked at Isla, her eyes widening. "Another cub?"

Isla nodded. "I think so."

"Wow!" Gracie whispered. "Two otter cubs! Let's follow these prints."

The two girls began to track the otter cub around the western side of Loch Dooey, being careful to stay back from the dangerous watery edge.

"This is strange," said Gracie. "The footprints go forwards then backwards again."

"The poor little thing is probably confused," said Isla. "And starving too."

A sudden noise startled them. They looked up as a large bird lifted its long, elegant body and soared into the steel-grey sky.

"It's a heron!" said Isla.

"He's dropped something," said Gracie, pointing to a shiny shape on the ground. "Look, it's a fish. Hey, Mr Heron!"

"He'll come back for it soon," said Isla.

They were just passing the remains of the old Roman fort when Isla grabbed Gracie by the hand. "Listen!"

Gracie stopped and grinned. "Is that what I think it is?"

"That's the sound I thought I heard this morning!" Isla cried. "It's definitely an otter cub."

The girls stood very still, listening and peering all around.

"There!" Gracie cried, pointing back towards the flooded Boggy Burn. The tiny otter cub was walking around, bewildered and yelping. Its long tail dragged along the ground. It was near the edge of the flooded wooden bridge that crossed the burn.

Isla looked through her binoculars. "It's the exact colour and size of our cub. I think it's his twin!"

"Wow! Double cuteness!" said Gracie.

"Double trouble more like!" said Isla. "This cub must have wandered further up the river from your house and ended up here." The girls began to walk slowly towards the bridge.

"So where's their mum?" asked Gracie.

"Mmm," said Isla, stopping a safe distance from the flood and the baby otter. "I'm not sure what happened, but I think they're orphans now."

"What should we do?" asked Gracie, and then she gasped. "Oh no! The cub looks like it's panicking! It's going to try to cross the burn!"

Sure enough, the tiny otter was taking steps towards the flooded bridge.

"One wrong move and the poor wee thing will be washed into the water," warned Isla. "It can't swim, remember!"

The otter cub turned and began to mew at Isla.

"It seems to like the sound of your voice, Isla – keep talking!" said Gracie.

Isla knelt down and said softly, "Stay there, little one! We'll get you to safety."

The otter seemed to do as it was told and stopped in its tracks.

"You keep talking," said Gracie, "and I'll run back to the lodge and get help."

"OK," agreed Isla. "But hurry! Go!"

But when Isla looked up, Gracie had already gone.

7

Back at the lodge, Lexi was sitting on the floor and staring into the baby otter's crate, working on her sketch. It was difficult to get the fluffiness of the cub's fur just right.

"That is *so cool*," said Buzz, looking over her shoulder.

"Thanks, Buzz," said Lexi, beaming. "What are you up to, by the way?"

"I was, um, just going to check how much bird food we have. I'll nip out to the shed."

"Do you want me to come, Buzz?" said Lisa. "I was about to start clearing the path around Pitten Pond, but I can help you first."

"No!" blurted Buzz.

Lisa frowned.

"I mean, no, it's OK, thanks." Buzz's voice was softer now. "The shed is a mess at the moment. I'm still sorting it out," he added with a nervous laugh.

"OK, I'll leave you to it!" said Lisa, heading out of the lodge.

"Lisa, I'll come and help you once I've finished my sketch," Lexi called after her.

Lexi pretended to add some shading to her drawing, but she was actually watching Buzz out of the corner of her eye. She had been counting how many times he'd been to the shed today: this was his *third* trip! What was he up to? A few seconds after Buzz left the lodge, Lexi stood up and followed, creeping quietly behind him.

Outside, at the back of the lodge, was

the big storage shed where the rangers kept tools, bird food, packs of loo rolls, paper towels and soap. The door was shut, but Lexi could hear something inside. She put her ear to the door and heard strange squeaking sounds and Buzz talking very softly! Who on earth was he speaking to? If only she could get a little closer... She pressed her ear as hard as she could against the door when, all of a sudden, Buzz opened it! Lexi tumbled onto the floor of the shed in a tangled heap.

"Woah!" she shouted.

"What are you doing?" said Buzz angrily, shutting the door behind her. "Spying on me?"

"I was just wondering why you kept coming out here," said Lexi, scrabbling around, trying to get to her feet. "And who were you talking to? It's so dark in here, I can't see a thing. And what is that disgusting smell?" She stood up and switched on the light. Suddenly she was aware of movement all over the floor. "Buzz, what on earth…?"

Mice! And they were *everywhere!* Startled by the light, they scampered into holes and disappeared.

Lexi looked at Buzz's scarlet face.

"What is going on?" she blurted, pinching her nose.

Buzz bit his lip. "It's not a big deal. What's wrong with a few mice?"

"A *few*?" gasped Lexi. "Buzz, there were loads. There's poo everywhere. It stinks!"

"OK, OK! Please, Lexi, don't tell Lisa or the rest of the Animal Adventure Club," he pleaded. "I started feeding some mice because I was worried about them. It's been raining for ages and I thought they might be struggling to find food."

"And what happened?" asked Lexi. "Did more appear?"

"*Yes!*" said Buzz, sounding utterly fed up. "More and more. And then *more.* They've eaten most of the bird food, and now they're chewing through toilet rolls and paper towels. They've made a huge mess! But I can't stop feeding them. They need me." He groaned.

"Oh Buzz, it's not that bad really," said Lexi. She looked around the shed. "OK, there are mouse droppings everywhere, the place pongs and they've eaten everything in sight, but..."

Buzz looked at Lexi doubtfully. "This had better be a good 'but', Lexi."

"But," said Lexi, "on the bright side, the mice have been having a ball!"

She let out a chuckle, and then a giggle, and before she knew it she was roaring with laughter, tears rolling down her cheeks.

"Oh Buzz," she said in between howls. "These mice have been having *way* too much fun in here! 'Free food guys, let's party!'" Lexi said in a squeaky Mickey Mouse voice. "'Tell all the mice in Pittendooey! Buzz says we're all invited!' I can just imagine them leaping and bouncing all over the place, swinging from the lights and having an awesome mouse party!"

The corners of Buzz's mouth curled up. "I suppose it is a bit funny... But what will Lisa say? She *hates* mice."

"I'll help you," said Lexi, wiping her eyes. "In my mum and dad's hotel, we had mice once in a storeroom and we managed to get rid of them."

"Without hurting them?"

"Yes," said Lexi. "We used special humane traps that don't hurt mice at all. But we'll have to tell everyone, you know. My granny says a problem shared is a problem halved. And with our club, it's a problem quartered!"

Buzz nodded slowly. "Thanks, Lexi. I've been so worried that I haven't been able to think about anything else."

"Buzz, we're a team. We look out for each other!" she said, giving Buzz a mini Animal Adventure Club fist bump. "What kind of mice are these anyway?"

"Long-tailed field mice," said Buzz, brightening up. He bent down to pick up an empty bag of birdseed and a mouse scampered out. It sniffed around boldly, its whiskers twitching. "That's Pipsqueak!" said Buzz. "She's my favourite. She's almost tame!"

Pipsqueak stopped in the middle of the floor. She had gleaming black, beady eyes, huge round ears and a tiny pink nose. She stood up on her back legs, washed her face with her tiny paws, then gave Buzz and Lexi a cheeky look and bolted away.

Just then, the door burst open and Gracie ran in.

"Thank goodness I've found you... Ugh! What's that smell?" she blurted. "Never mind, there's no time to explain. Where's the fishing net?"

"Here," said Buzz, unhooking the long net from the wall of the shed. He handed it quickly to Gracie.

"Come on," said Gracie. "There's another otter cub in danger!"

8

Isla watched helplessly as the tiny otter cub put a paw on the edge of the wooden bridge across the Boggy Burn. The rain was falling heavily. *Hurry up, Gracie!* she thought.

She glanced up and finally spotted Gracie sprinting along the path on the other side of the bridge, holding a large fishing net. Lexi and Buzz weren't far behind.

"Buzz!" Isla shouted over. "You stay on that side in case the cub tries to make a run for it."

Buzz stood on the other side of the

bridge and gave Isla a thumbs-up.

We've got the cub surrounded, thought Isla, *but we mustn't frighten it or it'll leap into the water.*

Gracie and Lexi carefully crossed the fallen tree and sped up to Isla.

"Use this," said Gracie, passing the net to Isla. "I think the cub trusts you, Isla. Try to get it to walk into the net!"

Isla nodded and slowly stepped closer to the baby otter. But the cub was startled and began to back away onto the watery bridge.

"We need bait to tempt it towards the net!" Buzz called.

"Fish!" said Gracie. "Lisa said our cub was the right age to start eating fish."

"But how are we going to catch a fish right now?" asked Lexi.

"I know!" Isla cried. "Remember the fish the heron dropped, Gracie? It looked like it was a brown trout, perfect for otters!"

"C'mon Lexi," said Gracie. "Help me find it."

"Yuck," grumbled Lexi. "I hate fish."

Gracie grabbed the net from Isla and they ran back up to the long grass.

"There it is!" said Gracie, pointing to the partly eaten fish on the grass.

"Ew," said Lexi. "It looks slimy. I'm not touching that!"

"Hurry!" They heard Buzz shouting in the distance. "The cub's on the bridge now!"

Lexi knelt down, shut her eyes and grasped the trout. It slipped around in her grip. "It feels *disgusting*," she complained.

"Here, put it in the net," Gracie said.

Lexi opened one eye and dropped it in.

"Good job, Lexi," said Gracie, sprinting away and leaving Lexi to wipe her fingers on the wet grass.

"We need to lay the net on the bridge," said Isla when Gracie arrived back. "The cub's about halfway over now. We need to encourage it to walk onto the net. Then we can scoop it up! It'll be tricky, but it's worth a shot."

"Good idea," called Buzz from the other side.

Gracie passed the net to Isla, who walked close to the bridge. She lay down on the muddy ground and stretched the handle of the net as far as she could. Gracie knelt down beside her. The net was long enough to stretch three quarters of the way over.

From both sides of the loch, the Animal

Adventure Club watched and waited. The otter cub lifted its nose to the air while the water lapped over its tiny paws.

"Don't be frightened, little one. Just a few more steps and you'll be safe," Isla called to the cub. It looked at her with its big brown eyes and cocked its head, as if it really was listening to her. It lifted a paw...

Suddenly a gush of water caught the little otter by surprise and washed it close to the edge of the bridge. The gang gasped. The otter cub whined loudly but managed to balance itself.

"I can't watch," said Lexi, closing her eyes.

Isla stretched her body so that the net was even closer to the little otter's paws. Her arms ached, and although she wanted to shuffle further forwards, she knew she had to put her own safety first. It would be dangerous to move any nearer to the water's edge. Suddenly a wave of worry washed over her.

"What if this doesn't work?" she whispered. "What if I just can't save the cub?"

"We can only do our best, Isla," Gracie said. "We can't save every animal in the world, or even every animal in Pittendooey! But we can try. Remember, the Animal Adventure Club is with you. We're a team!"

Isla stared at the shivering otter cub, who was only millimetres from the water's edge. "Thanks, Gracie," Isla said, and she stretched her arms as far as she could.

The cub, who had smelled the fish at last, began to shuffle towards the net.

"Look!" said Gracie. "It's coming closer."

"Get ready to help me lift the net, guys," said Isla.

Gracie and Lexi knelt beside Isla and grabbed the handle.

"It's nearly there!" said Lexi.

"Just a few more wee steps!" said Gracie.

Suddenly the heron swooped past. The

little otter let out a terrified yelp and lost its balance. Instinctively, Isla tilted the net, nudged the cub – and it tipped in!

"Now!" said Isla, and she, Gracie and Lexi hauled the net up into the air. The otter cub let out frantic yelping squeaks as it found itself flying.

"Wowza!" shouted Lexi. "You've caught the cub! You did it!"

"*We* did it!" Isla corrected her.

"No thanks to Mr Heron sticking his beak in when it wasn't wanted!" called Buzz.

"He must've spotted his fish," said Lexi.

Together they looked at the otter cub, safe inside the net but still chattering with fright. Gracie reached in very carefully to remove the fish.

"Let's get this little one to the lodge to

see its twin!" Gracie beamed. "Here Lexi, catch!" She tossed the trout to Lexi, who reached out before she realised what it was.

"Ew, not again!" laughed Lexi, clutching the fish.

"Can you carry it back to the lodge?" said Isla. "If we mush it up a bit, we can feed it to our wee cubs."

Lexi held the trout by its tail fin at arm's length and pinched her nose with her other hand. "The things I do for this club," she sighed.

"Excellent teamwork, guys," said Isla.

"Easy, eh?" Gracie laughed. "This cub is almost more adorable than the other one!"

"I'll run ahead and warn Lisa. She'll be surprised!" yelled Buzz from the other side of the burn. "The poor wee thing must be *starving*. I know I am. I think this calls for a celebratory round of custard creams!"

9

Back in the lodge, Lisa carefully took the otter cub out of the net. "Well, well, well," she said with a chuckle. "Another boy too!"

She dried him with a towel, making his fur even fluffier, and then gently popped him into the crate with his brother. Everyone gathered round to watch. At first the two otters seemed wary of each other, but soon they were chattering and whistling together.

"That is so sweet," said Gracie.

"Lots of play and interaction is what this pair needs. Otter cubs thrive on it!" Lisa explained.

"What about putting some toys in there for them?" said Buzz, and he rummaged around in the cupboards. He found a couple of balls and popped them in the crate. The otter cubs began pushing the balls around with their paws and noses, squealing and purring all the time.

"Did you know," said Isla, who was looking up facts on the computer, "that a group of otters on land is called a 'romp'? But if they're in the water, it's a 'raft'."

"I love that," said Buzz. "They're certainly romping now!"

The two otters were bounding around the crate together, chasing the balls.

"I'll make up the next batch of bottles," said Gracie with a sigh. "Looking after twins really is exhausting. You feed one and get it settled, then you've got the other one to feed."

"Pitt and Dooey. Pitt and Dooey! I've got it!" said Isla all of a sudden.

"What are you talking about?" asked Lexi.

"That's what we should call the otter twins," said Isla, coming over to the crate.

"One is Pitt, the other is Dooey. Pitt 'n' Dooey! Get it?" The otters both squeaked and put their front paws up against the crate.

Everyone fell about laughing. "Brilliant," said Lexi.

"Ooh, they like their names!" said Gracie. The two otter cubs were staring at everyone with their heads tilted to one side. "But which is which?"

"Pitt is the one with the lighter patch on his chin, see?" said Lexi, looking closely at the fluffy cubs.

"Hey, I almost forgot," Gracie said to Lexi. "What were you and Buzz doing in the shed earlier? And what was that terrible smell?"

Buzz shifted around uncomfortably.

"Oh, well," said Lexi, looking awkwardly

at Buzz. "It was nothing, really."

"It's OK, Lexi," said Buzz, his face bright red. "I need to tell everyone."

Buzz explained about the mice and how he'd been feeding them.

"It started with some crusts of bread, but then it got out of control," he said sheepishly. "I'm so sorry for all the mess they've made, Lisa."

"The mice that live around the nature reserve are not really pets," said Lisa with her eyebrows raised.

"I know, I know," said Buzz. "I suppose I thought that because we feed the birds, why not feed the mice too?"

"But birds stay outside, don't they, Buzz," said Lisa quietly. "Mice chew through wires, and they wee and poo everywhere."

"And they multiply very quickly," added Gracie.

"And they eat their way through any kind of food that's lying around. Like big sacks of birdseed," said Buzz, dropping his head. "They've eaten most of it."

"Oops," said Lexi, trying to lighten the mood. "But on the plus side, they've had plenty of food to keep them going through this bad weather."

"I wouldn't be surprised if they've built themselves a nice cosy nest right under the shed. Sounds like they've got a great wee set-up!" said Lisa.

"There's a moose loose about this hoose!" said Isla, chuckling.

"Make that, 'There's mice in the shed scoffing birdseed and bread!'" quipped Gracie.

Lexi snorted with laughter.

"I'm so sorry," said Buzz, looking ashamed of himself. "I should've remembered that sharing a problem really helps solve it! Teamwork really is the best way."

"But you were just being kind, Buzz," said Isla. "You were putting the animals first, like you always do."

"Don't be so hard on yourself," said Lisa. "As you long as you've learned from this, that's the main thing."

"I'll help Buzz move the mice on," said Lexi.

"We'll all help!" said Isla. The Animal Adventure Club leaned in for one of their special fist bumps.

"Getting rid of any food that's left would be a good start," said Gracie.

"Humane mouse traps would be ideal, but the ones I ordered for the lodge haven't arrived yet," said Lisa.

"We've got some spares at home," said Lexi. "We can trap the mice without hurting them and then release them on the other side of the nature reserve."

"And then we can block up any mouse holes to stop them getting back in," added Gracie.

air holes

door spring

peanut butter

"Right, let's get that shed *squeaky* clean," said Isla, standing up. "Get it?"

"Oof, that's so *cheesy*, Isla," said Buzz with a cheeky smile.

"Hey, what's a mouse's favourite game?" said Lexi. "*Hide and squeak!*"

"Ugh," they all groaned as they headed out to the shed. Lisa followed, helping to carry dustpans and brushes.

As Isla opened the door of the shed, mice darted in every direction.

"Aargh!" Lisa shrieked. "On second thoughts, I need to crack on with feeding Pitt 'n' Dooey!" she shouted, and scuttled off back inside the lodge.

"It was *mice* seeing you, Lisa!" said Buzz.

The mice scattered as the Animal Adventure Club swept out the shed, but one little mouse stood still in the middle of the floor and looked up at Buzz hopefully. Buzz knelt down and spoke gently.

"The party's over now, Pipsqueak. Off you go."

And the tiny mouse turned and ran off into the woods.

10

Lexi flopped onto the sofa in the lodge. "Well, the shed's tidy. We've swept, we've scrubbed, we've taken away any food that was left and we've blocked any wee holes with steel wool for now. I'll ask Mum and Dad to give you their spare humane mouse traps, Lisa."

"And we'll find any wee mice that wander into them a nice new home far away from the lodge," added Gracie.

"Boo!" said Buzz in a pretend sad voice. "But I'm going to put everything I've learned about mice in a special Animal Adventure Club mouse fact sheet.

I'll miss Pipsqueak though," he added forlornly.

"Don't worry, Buzz. I'll draw a picture of her for you," Lexi offered. Buzz smiled.

"Great idea! Gracie and I can write a fact sheet about the otters, to go with Lexi's fab sketches of Pitt 'n' Dooey," said Isla.

"Thanks, Isla," beamed Lexi.

"By the way, while we were cleaning out the shed we found this old basin," said Gracie, popping it on the floor near the crate. "We thought it would be nice for the cubs to have a wee paddle."

She began filling it with jugfuls of water while Pitt and Dooey watched, intrigued. Lisa helped to lift the otter twins out of the crate and popped them on the floor beside the basin. Just then, her phone began to ring. She headed over to her desk to answer it.

"Look at Pitt!" said Lexi. The little cub began tapping the surface of the water with one paw, and then he slid his whole body into the water. He looked very pleased with himself.

"Aw!" said Lexi.

"That is super cute!" said Buzz.

Lisa walked back over. "Well, that was the wildlife hospital on the phone. The floods have gone down, and the road to Strathdooey is clear now! I said I'd pop over with our otter cubs."

"Oh no!" said Lexi. "I'm not ready to say goodbye to Pitt 'n' Dooey!"

"You've done a great job, Animal Adventure Club!" said Lisa. "These little otters might not have survived without you."

"I wonder what happened to their mother?" asked Isla.

"She might have been out hunting for food when the flood flushed Pitt and Dooey out of their holt," said Lisa. "They were probably washed ashore."

"That's so sad," said Buzz.

The otter cubs both let out little squeaks.

"Don't worry," said Lisa. "The team at the wildlife hospital will look after them until they're ready to go back out into the wild."

"Do you think we can go and visit them?" asked Gracie.

"I'm sure you can," said Lisa. "But soon they'll stop handling them, so that they don't get too used to humans." She turned to the kitchen counter and picked up a bowl. "Let's make sure they're well fed before they go. I've mushed up the trout you found earlier and mixed it with some formula."

She popped the bowl into the crate and the two cubs were soon nibbling at the fish.

"Their very first fish supper," said Buzz.

"What a mess!" laughed Gracie. Both

the otter cubs' faces were covered in the milky fish. "Yuk, I don't fancy eating fish for a while!"

"Me neither," added Lexi with a shudder. "Hey, look – Dooey's falling asleep!"

Sure enough, the little otter cub's eyes began to close and he started to sway. Then, with a thump, he fell head first into the bowl of fish mush.

Everyone burst out laughing.

"It's been quite a day for them," said Lisa. "They must be exhausted. When Pitt's finished, I'll get them cosied up in their crate, then put them in the van. They can have a good sleep on the way to the wildlife hospital."

"Right everyone," said Isla, looking at her phone, "my mum's just texted to say she's finally heading home and is going to take us all out for tea! Who's in?"

"Me!" said Buzz, already texting his mum.

"Yay!" agreed Gracie.

"And me!" added Lexi.

"Awesome," said Isla. "Lisa?"

"Thanks, Isla, but I've got my hands full with these little guys," said Lisa. "Say your goodbyes to Pitt 'n' Dooey."

"Aw, goodbye wee things, we'll come and see you soon," said Isla.

Soon Isla's mum was helping to throw anoraks and rucksacks into the boot and the Animal Adventure Club were piling into her car.

Isla threw her arms around her mum's neck and planted a big kiss on her cheek. "It's so good to see you, Mum," said Isla.

"I've missed you too," said Mum, giving Isla a squeeze. "Thank goodness the rain's stopped! I thought I'd never get home."

She turned to Buzz, Gracie and Lexi. "Right, Animal Adventure Club, what do you fancy for tea? What about a fish supper?"

Buzz wrinkled his nose and Gracie put her hand over her mouth. Lexi blurted, "Oh no, not more FISH!"

Isla's mum looked puzzled and Isla

giggled. "Don't worry, Mum, we'll explain on the way. But I'm not sure any of us can face any more fish for a while!"

"Could we go for pizza instead?" Buzz asked.

"That would be otterly fantastic, Mum!" said Isla. Gracie, Lexi and Buzz burst out laughing.

Isla's mum laughed too as she drove out of the car park. "I haven't got a clue what you're giggling about, but you can tell me about it over pizza. C'mon Animal Adventure Club, I want to hear all about what you've been up to!"

The End

Come exploring with the

ANIMAL
Adventure Club

ANIMAL ADVENTURE CLUB CODE

MEMBERS:

Isla MacLeod

Buzz (Robert) Campbell

Gracie Munroe

Lexi Budge

OUR MISSION IS TO TAKE CARE OF ALL LIVING CREATURES.

CODE

1. We will treat all animals from bugs to badgers with respect. Even midges and spiders!

2. We will look after the natural world and respect the countryside.

3. We will never drop litter.

And we'll recycle any we find lying around.

4. We will have fun outdoors!

5. We will always work as a team.

6. We will deal with problems calmly and come up with a sensible plan.

7. We will ask adults for advice when we need to.

8. We will always be prepared and pack a torch, map, compass and waterproof jacket before going on patrol.

9. We will always welcome new members.

10. We will always have hot chocolate and a packet of biscuits in the lodge.

Preferably custard creams!

SIGNED:

Buzz   Isla

Gracie   Lexi

How to make an origami bat

The Animal Adventure Club made bat arts and crafts for their Bat Chat. Make your own origami bat!

You will need...

- Square of black paper
- Scissors
- Pencil
- Stick-on googly eyes (optional)
- Thread

1. Take your square of black paper and fold one corner over to the opposite corner to make a triangle.

2. Turn the triangle round so the long straight edge is at the top and fold the top third down. The bottom of the paper will look like a V shape.

It looks like an upside-down boat!

3. To make the bat's wings, take the top left corner and fold it right to the bottom of the V. Repeat this with the top right corner to make the other wing.

4. Gently unfold the wings, and then bend each one in about a centimetre.

5. Flip your bat over.

6. Take your scissors and make a snip down and along the top of its head to create two wee triangles for ears. You can draw these with a pencil first if you like.

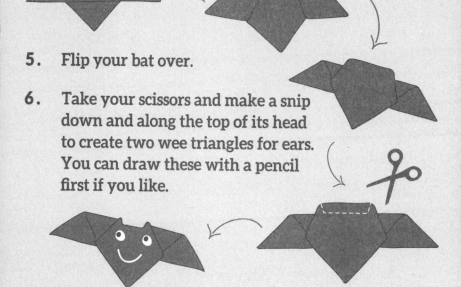

7. Draw on some funny eyes or (if you have them) stick on googly eyes. You can stick a bit of thread on the back and hang your bat in your bedroom!

How to make a rain gauge

Have you ever wondered exactly how much rain falls?
Here's a simple gadget you can make out of a recycled
plastic bottle to measure it.

You will need...

- 2 litre recycled plastic bottle
- Scissors
- Ruler
- Permanent marker pen

1. Take the lid off the plastic bottle,
   and remove the label too.

2. Cut off the top section of the bottle, about one third
   of the way down.

   *This can be tricky.
   Ask a grown-up for help if you need it.*

3. Turn the top section upside down and fit it inside
   the bottle to make a funnel.

4. Hold your ruler against the bottle and use a permanent marker pen to draw on measurements in centimetres from the bottom up.

5. Stick your rain gauge in some soil so it doesn't blow over, but make sure the funnel sticks out about 5cm.

6. Wait for some rainfall.

   You won't have to wait long!

7. When the rain stops, carefully lift your rain gauge out of the ground and check the measurements to see how much rain has fallen.

8. Try keeping a weather chart to track how much rain falls on different days. Check your rain gauge at the same time every day, write down the measurement, then empty out the bottle ready for next time.

9. Add up all your measurements to see how much rain falls in a week, or a month, or even a year!

European Otter

Male = Boar
Female = Sow
Babies = Cubs or Pups

What do we look like?
- We have thick brown and white fur, webbed feet and a powerful tail called a rudder.
- We have five toes on our paws.

Where do we live?
- Different kinds of otters live all over the world, except Australia and Antarctica.
- Otters found in Britain and Europe are called *Lutra lutra*.
- You can find us in rivers, wetlands and along the coast.
- Our homes are underground burrows called 'holts'.
- Our resting places, on the banks of rivers, are called 'couches'.

What do we like to eat?

- We eat fish, water birds, insects, crustaceans and amphibians.

Otter footprints

What do we sound like?

- We make lots of different noises!
- We chirp when we want to find each other.
- We grunt or snarl when we're cross.
- We hiss or yelp when we're worried.
- We purr and squeal when we're playing!

Fun facts

How cool is that?

- We are shy animals.
- We don't know how to swim when we're babies. Our mums teach us when we're about 10 weeks old.
- We can close our noses and ears when we swim underwater.
- Our droppings are called spraints. They contain fish bones and smell like jasmine tea!

Pipistrelle Bat

Babies = Pups

What do we look like?
- We have golden-brown fur, which is paler underneath and darker around our faces.
- We are really small – only 3 to 5cm long! But our wingspan is 20cm.
- We are the smallest bat in the UK. We weigh less than a 50p coin!

Where do we live?
- You can find us all over Britain, except in the Shetland Islands and parts of Orkney.
- We like to roost in trees, but you can also find us in buildings like churches or in underground places like caves, cellars and under bridges.

What do we like to eat?
- We eat insects like moths, midges, flies, beetles and spiders.
- We can eat 3,000 insects every night!

wowza!

What do we sound like?
- We make noises that are too high-pitched for you to hear. But our calls are very useful to us: the echoes that bounce back help us hunt for food and avoid flying into things. It's called echolocation and is very clever.

Fun facts
- We are the only mammals that fly.
- We are nocturnal, but you might see us out hunting at dusk or dawn.
- We can live up to 5 years.
- We hibernate over the cold winter months, when insects are tricky to find.

Long-tailed Field Mouse

Male = Buck
Female = Doe
Babies = Pups or Pinkies

This is because they're pink when they're born.

So cute!

What do we look like?
- We have sandy-brown fur and a whitish-grey belly.
- We have large eyes and ears.
- Our tails can grow as long as 9cm!

Where do we live?
- You can find us all over Europe. We are the most common mouse in the UK.

There are 38 million in Britain!

- We live in woodland, grassland and gardens. Our burrows are underground.
- If the weather is bad and we're looking for food, we explore buildings or sheds.

I know ••

What do we like to eat?

- We eat seeds, nuts, buds and berries, but also caterpillars, worms and snails.
- We store our food underground and sometimes in old birds' nests.

Field mouse footprints

What do we sound like?

- We squeak and chirp.
- You might also hear us scurrying around or gnawing our food!

Fun facts

- We are also known as wood mice.
- We are very fast and good climbers.
- We can shed the end of our tail if it gets trapped, but it might not grow back.
- When we're foraging, we leave twigs as wee signposts to remind us where to find food.

What if I find an injured wild animal?

The Animal Adventure Club have lots of exciting encounters with wild animals, but remember that in real life you should always ask a grown-up for help. If you find an injured wild animal, call a local vet or wildlife organisation for advice.

Top Tips

- Be sensible and cautious. Stay back and watch the animal for a while to see how badly injured it is. Wild animals can scratch and bite.

- Tell a grown-up, or call a vet or wildlife organisation for help.

- If you are helping a grown-up collect a wild animal, you can suggest that they line a well-ventilated cardboard box with newspaper or towels. Next, put on gloves, lift the animal (keeping it away from your face), and quickly put it into the box.

- There are some injured animals you should never try to handle: deer, seals, wild boar, otters, badgers, foxes, snakes, birds of prey (including owls), swans, geese, herons or gulls. Instead, call a vet or wildlife organisation.